The Mo

S0-ADP-348

523.3 LLE   Llewellyn, Claire

STARTERS

The Moon

Claire Llewellyn

First published by Hodder Wayland
338 Euston Road, London NW1 3BH, United Kingdom
Hodder Wayland is an imprint of Hodder Children's
Books, a division of Hodder Headline Limited.

This edition published under license from Hodder
Children's Books. All rights reserved.
Text copyright © Claire Llewellyn 2003

Design: Perry Tate Design, Language consultant: Andrew Burrell,
Science consultant: Dr. Carol Ballard

Published in the United States by Smart Apple Media
1980 Lookout Drive, North Mankato, MN 56003

Library of Congress Cataloging-in-Publication Data

Llewellyn, Claire.
The moon / by Claire Llewellyn. p. cm. — (Starters)
Contents: The night sky — Earth's neighbor — The moon's orbit — The light of the
moon — The shape of the moon — Moon watching — On the moon — Going to the
moon — Walking on the moon — Leaving the moon.
ISBN 1-58340-260-8 1. Moon—Juvenile literature. [1. Moon.] I. Title. II. Series.
QB582.L64 2003 523.3—dc21   2003041519

9 8 7 6 5 4 3 2 1

The publishers would like to thank the following for permission to reproduce
photographs in this book: Science Photo Library, title page, contents page, 6-9, 11,
15-18 (top), 19, 22, 24 (bottom 3 pictures) / Bruce Coleman, cover, 5, 10, 12-14 /
Genesis, 18 (right), 21, 24 (top) / Galaxy Pictures, 23

Contents

The night sky

When you look up at the sky on a clear night, you are looking into space.

Millions of stars twinkle in the darkness, but the Moon looks much brighter than any star. It is the brightest object in the sky.

The Moon looks big in the night sky.

Earth's neighbor

We live on a planet called Earth, a giant rocky ball that spins in space. The Moon is our nearest neighbor.

The Earth is four times bigger than the Moon.

6

But the Moon is still a long way away. If you could drive a car to the Moon, it would take more than half a year!

A rocket takes three days to get to the Moon.

Saturn

Some of Saturn's moons

Many other planets have moons, too. Saturn has many moons. Earth has only one.

The Moon's orbit

The Moon is a rocky ball, just like the Earth, and it is always moving. It travels around and around the Earth, following a path called an orbit.

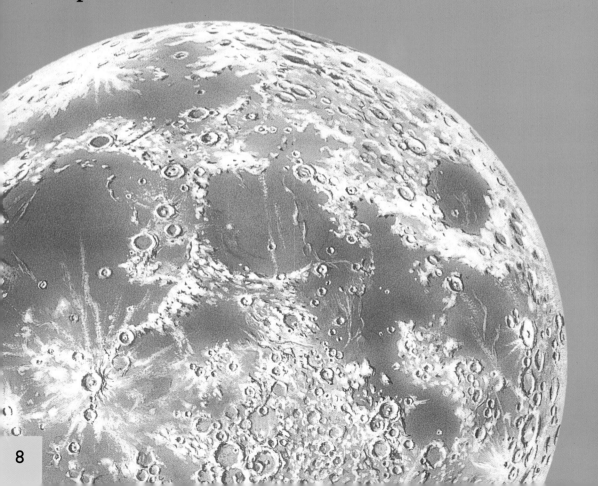

8

The Moon takes 28 days to orbit the Earth.

The Earth and the Moon belong to the Solar System, a **BIG** family of planets and moons that travel around the Sun.

9

The light of the Moon

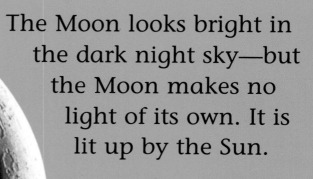

The Moon looks bright in the dark night sky—but the Moon makes no light of its own. It is lit up by the Sun.

We can only see the part of the Moon that is lit up by the Sun.

The Sun's light hits the Moon and bounces down to the Earth. To us, this light looks very pale. We call it moonlight.

Moonlight is soft
and silvery, but
on some nights it
helps us to see.

The shape of the Moon

A crescent moon

A half moon

As the Moon travels around the Earth, its shape appears to change. Each night, it looks a little bit different than the way it looked the night before.

For 14 nights, the Moon seems to grow bigger and bigger until it is a huge round ball. Then, for 14 nights, it seems to get smaller again until we see nothing at all.

A full moon

If you use a telescope or binoculars, you can see the Moon's surface clearly.

The surface is covered
with holes called
craters, which are
wide and very
deep. They were
made when huge
rocks hurtled through
space and crashed into
the Moon.

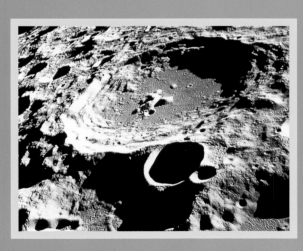

These dark
patches are
flat areas.

These light
patches are
rocky
mountains.

There is no water or air on the Moon. There are no clouds, and no wind or rain. Nothing can grow or live there—not a single animal or plant.

By day, the Moon is boiling hot. By night, it is freezing cold.

The Moon's sky
is always black.

Going to the Moon

Astronauts have traveled to the Moon in a rocket. They wore spacesuits to protect them from the heat and the cold, and to give them a supply of air.

The astronauts took a SMALLER spacecraft down to the Moon itself.

The Moon landings helped scientists to find out all sorts of things, such as how old the Moon is and how it was made.

The astronauts collected rocks for scientists to study.

Walking on the Moon

Walking on the Moon looks fun.
The astronauts could take **giant** steps
and bounce high off the ground.

On Earth, an invisible force called gravity keeps us on the ground. Gravity is not as **strong** on the Moon, so people feel much lighter.

You weigh a lot less on the Moon.

You can jump a lot higher, too.

21

Leaving the Moon

The astronauts returned to their rocket and traveled back to Earth. They left behind a flag and lots of footprints on the surface.

You can see the planet Earth in this picture of the Moon.

We do not know when people will return to the Moon. Maybe one day, scientists will build a space station there and we will all be able to visit the Moon.

Glossary and index